This Book Belongs to

....

Produced by Cat's Pyjamas
1A London Road, Enfield,
Middlesex, EN2 6BN
www.catspyjamasbooks.com
Cat's Pyjamas is an imprint of Fernleigh Books Ltd.

ISBN 978-1-906293-66-6
Printed in China

Five Minute Collection

Bedtime
Bunny Tales

Too Many Guests To Feed

Laura and Lizzy were twins, and it was their birthday. Mum said they could have a small party, with family and only a couple of friends each.

But the twins were much too excited and invited everyone they could think of! They invited all their class and then all their classes' brothers, sisters and friends. So on the day of the party hundreds of bunnies turned up.

"We can't possibly have the party now!" said Mum angrily. "There isn't enough food to go around!"

Laura and Lizzy were very upset, their guests looked very hungry and now the party would have to end before it had even started!

At that moment Uncle David and Aunty Lou arrived.

"We've got a surprise for you!" said Aunty Lou as Uncle David carried in a GIANT birthday cake, big enough for everyone!

"Thanks!" cried the twins. "Now we can have our party after all!"

Rachel's Special Stars

Rachel didn't like bedtime. "Read me another story," she would ask.

"Can I have another glass of water?"

But really Rachel was just scared of the dark.

"Come with me," said Mum taking Rachel's paw and leading her to the big window. "I'll show you something very special."

She pointed up to the sky and Rachel saw the huge, silver moon and millions of stars twinkling above.

"See how beautiful it is!" Mum said. "Even when the lights are out and Dad and I have gone to bed, the stars and moon stay up just to keep watch over you. They shine brightly every night to make sure you are snuggled up safely!"

Rachel climbed back into bed and burrowed down under the covers. She looked thoughtful for a minute, but then she smiled and gave Mum the biggest hug she could.

"Night, night, Mum," she said as she closed her eyes. "I don't feel so scared now that I know the stars are shining for me!"

Graffiti In The Playground

James was always getting into trouble for drawing. He drew all the time, even when he should have been doing his schoolwork or going to bed! But worse, he drew everywhere! He drew on the walls, the floor, even on the ceiling!

Something had to be done. His teacher Mrs Burrows had an idea.

"The playground needs brightening up," she told James, "so why don't you do an enormous painting on the wall of the school? This is the proper time and place to paint on the wall!"

James thought it was a great idea and worked very hard on the planning and painting. Eventually the painting was finished and it looked fantastic. Everyone was very proud of their new colourful school, and of their school artist, James!

Following The Clues

It was raining and Mum said that Edward had to stay indoors. Edward spent the morning watching his favourite show, 'Detective Columbobunny'.

"I bet I could be a detective!" he boasted to his sister, Olivia. "In fact, I think I'd be the best one in the world! It's all about following the clues!"

For the rest of the day Edward played detective. He found Olivia in the hall.

"You're going shopping with Mum!" he said proudly. "You have an umbrella and you're carrying Mum's purse."

"Anyone could have worked that out!" answered Olivia. "Now remember to stay inside and don't get into any trouble!"

When Olivia came home she found Edward in the kitchen.

"You've been playing outside!" Olivia cried.

"How did you know?" asked Edward. "Did you see my wet coat in the cupboard? Or did I leave fingerprints on the door handle?"

"No," laughed Olivia. "Footprints! You're trailing mud all over the house! I think I'm a much better detective than you!"

We're Not Going Inside!

Jack and Jenny were sulking. They'd had a lovely holiday but tomorrow school started again. When they arrived home they refused to get out the car.

"We're not going inside until you take us back on holiday!" they wailed.

"All right!" said their mum and dad as they got out the car and went inside. Soon Jenny and Jack could smell dinner cooking.

"We're not going inside until they take us back!" said Jack.

They could see Dad watching TV through the window.

"We're not going!" said Jack.

"I wonder what's on TV?" said Jenny thoughtfully.

"I hope they leave us some dinner," said Jack hungrily.

"Look! Carrot burgers!" cried Jack. "My favourite!" And he quickly jumped out the car and ran inside at great speed.

"Wait for me!" called Jenny running in after him.

Bronco Bunny-The-Kid

"Yeehaw! Ride 'em cowboy!" yelled Cowbunny Josh clinging tightly to the reins. He waved his hat to the crowd as the bucking bronco reared and tossed its head. His leather waistcoat, spotted scarf and plaid shirt flapped as he bounced in the saddle and his shiny belt buckle flashed under the arena lights.

Josh was the king of the rodeo, the best showman and rider in the whole Wild West and very proud of himself! The crowd cheered and yelled loudly as Josh lasted longer on the horse than any other cowboy could. Josh could never be beaten. Until…

"Thump!"

"What was that noise?" asked Mum peering round the door.

"I fell off my horse!" moaned Josh sitting up and rubbing his bottom.

"You mean my sofa!" laughed Mum.

"Sorry!" said Josh. "But if I practise maybe one day I'll really be a rodeo star!"

The Joke's On Alfie!

Grandad Bunny was planning to teach young Alfie a lesson. Alfie loved playing tricks on him. At the moment his favourite was ringing Grandad's doorbell and then running off.

"I'll show him!" thought Grandad as he put on a fox mask and waited.

Sure enough soon Alfie rang the doorbell. In the blink of an eye Grandad jumped out from his hiding place. "Grrrrr!" he growled ferociously.

Alfie froze and burst into tears. A fox had eaten Grandad, and he was next!

Grandad took off his mask and gave Alfie a hug.

"I'm sorry to scare you," he said. "But I'm tired of you playing tricks on me!" Alfie had learnt his lesson with Grandad. But he did borrow the fox mask and he growled at all the passers-by on his way home!

Emily's Special Outfit

Emily hated the rain! She couldn't understand why all the other bunnies were so keen to splash around in the puddles.

"It messes up your fur and is so wet!" she thought. "What's the fun of that?"

Whenever it rained Emily would sit at the window and stare grumpily out at all the bunnies playing. Harry would take out a tiny boat and float it on the puddles while Charlie made waves for it. Ella and Lily would jump the puddles and occasionally land in one! But Emily wouldn't go out and join them no matter how much her friends called.

One day Mum came home with a special parcel for Emily. She unwrapped a beautiful shiny red raincoat and matching boots.

"These are for you so that you can go out and not get the slightest bit wet!" Mum said, smiling. Emily smiled too - they were so very red and shiny.

Now Emily is always the first one outside when it starts to rain!

Wonderful Robot Rabbit

Professor Wabbit could invent anything. He was the cleverest bunny in the whole of Warren Fields. His latest invention was Robot Rabbit.

"This robot can do anything I ask it!" said the professor. With the push of a button the robot was cutting the lawn, making sandwiches, dusting the house, painting the front door, washing the dishes and even fetching the newspaper!

"It can do much more than that!" said the professor. "Anything we can do, the robot can do too! Better and faster and for longer!"

"Can it hop?" asked Ruby Rabbit innocently. The professor thought very hard and pressed some buttons. The robots began to sway from side to side but then it fell to the floor with a CRASH!

"It can't hop, I'm afraid!" replied the professor thoughtfully. "I didn't think of that when I made it!"

"But all bunnies can hop!" laughed Ruby.

"When I fix Robot Rabbit he will too!" smiled Professor Wabbit.

A New View Of The World

Everyone knew that Rachel dreamed about flying high in the sky. She would lie on her back, watch the birds soaring above, then close her eyes and wish that one day she would be able to look down on her garden as they did.

One morning she woke up and found a note by her bed. It said,

"Come to the garden and make your dreams come true."

Rachel crept outside. A yellow ladder hung from the tallest oak tree. There she found another note.

"Climb up!" it said.

At the top she found a little tree house, painted green and hidden amongst the leaves. Inside was a final note, which said:

"Sorry we can't help you to fly, but instead we've made you this house. Now you can look down on the garden just like the birds! Love Mum and Dad."

Christmas Hide and Seek

For the whole month before Christmas the Bunny children searched high and low for their Christmas presents. They searched cupboards, corners, drawers, the attic and even Dad's shed but they couldn't find where Mum had hidden them. By Christmas Eve they still hadn't found them.

"Maybe we aren't getting any presents this year," said Ella. "Maybe we haven't been good enough bunnies!"

"Then Father Christmas will forget us too!" wailed Charlie, the youngest. The bunnies went to bed that night very sad, sure that Christmas was going to be a miserable time for them.

But in the morning they had such a surprise! There were lots of presents, all sizes and all shapes! Even their stockings were full to bursting!

Mum laughed at their shocked faces.

"Happy Christmas! You didn't think we'd forget you, did you? You'll never guess where I hid your presents! And I'm going to use the same place next year!"

The Red Carpet Treatment

One morning, Ethan and Amelia were watching TV when a special news story came on. It was all about the opening of a new film. There was a red carpet and lots of famous celebrities in beautiful clothes signing autographs. The crowds were excitedly cheering as cameras flashed.

"I wish I could be a celebrity!" sighed Ethan.

"We can always pretend," smiled Amelia. "We can invite all our friends and have our own autograph signing!"

So Ethan dressed up in his best clothes and pretended to be a famous movie star. All his friends cheered and clapped.

"Can we have your autograph please?" they asked him most politely. Ethan signed each rabbit's piece of paper and even wrote each one of them a special message!

When all his friends had gone Ethan collapsed on the armchair. "I don't think I want to be a star anymore," he sighed. "All this writing makes my paws ache!"

The Multi-coloured Bunny

Isabelle was the most colourful rabbit of them all. She would wear all the colours of the rainbow! Every morning she put on a red ribbon, orange jumper, yellow scarf, green skirt, blue socks, indigo shoes and violet gloves!

"I'm the brightest bunny there is!" she would boast.

One day Mum asked Isabelle if she would like to make some cookies with rainbow sprinkles.

"Yes please!" said Isabelle reaching up to get the sprinkles. Suddenly a large bag of flour fell out and covered Isabelle from top to toe. Her rainbow clothes disappeared in a dusty, white cloud.

"Oops!" said Mum. "What a mess!"

"I'm white all over!" cried Isabelle, looking down at herself. Her face and whiskers were white, her fluffy ears were white, and her clothes were white right down to her shoes!

"You're not so colourful today!" said Mum.

"Nevermind!" said Isabelle. "White makes a nice change!"

Digging, Digging, Digging!

Jacob loved to dig and he did it as much as he could! He would dig in the garden, by the lake, and in the wood. The other animals had to be careful not to fall down the many holes he made!

One day Jacob was digging by the Squirrel family's old oak tree.

"Why do you dig everywhere?" asked the littlest squirrel.

"It's what rabbits do best!" replied Jacob. "Except hopping that is!" Happy with this answer the littlest squirrel left him to it.

The next morning Jacob was still digging. Mrs Squirrel and all the little squirrels came out to say hello and see how he was getting on.

"It's very difficult to dig here!" he told her. "There are lots of nuts and acorns buried and they keep getting in my way!"

"Those are our winter food stores!" she replied.

"I'm very sorry!" said Jacob shyly. "I didn't think. I'd better put them back!"

"Then for once you will be burying things not digging them up!" Mrs Squirrel laughed, and Jacob had to laugh too!

Look Before you Leap

Alex was the fastest runner in his class. He thought he was the best jumper too!

"I bet I can jump higher than you!" he boasted to his friend Luke.

"We'll see!" replied Luke. "Why don't we have a competition?"

Alex thought this was a great chance to show off. "Let's jump up onto that bird table," he said.

With a running start Luke easily leapt up onto the bird table.

"Your go now!" he cried as he climbed down.

Alex sprang as high as he could. He jumped so high he nearly jumped *over* the bird table!

"Help!" he shouted clutching at the edge, "I'm going to fall!"

Luke quickly gathered together a pile of soft grass for Alex to fall on.

"You win!" said Alex once he was down. "I think I'll stick to running. I prefer keeping my feet safely on the ground!"

One Rabbit's Rubbish...

Chloe collected all sorts of interesting things from the junk heap. One day she found a large boot in a very pretty shade of yellow.

"I'll take it home and put it with the other things I've found," she smiled.

But when Chloe got home Mum was not very happy.

"Not another piece of old rubbish!" she said. "That boot wouldn't be useful to anybody! Take it back where you found it!"

On her way back she met a mouse family carrying bags and suitcases.

"What's the matter?" she asked them.

"Our house isn't big enough for all of us, and it'll be winter soon!" sobbed the biggest mouse, sniffing. Suddenly Chloe had an idea.

"Why don't you use this boot?" she suggested. "If we clean it up and add a roof it'll be a lovely snug place for winter!"

The mice were so happy with their new home that they invited everyone to a party, and Chloe was the guest of honour.

A Lucky Escape For Baby

Millie was now a big sister! Her mum had just bought home a sweet, little baby girl. Everyone peeped in at her small, furry face and tried to think of names.

"What about Evie?" said Dad.

"I've always liked the name Megan," said Mum.

But no-one could agree and soon they had run out of names!

Later that day, Millie and Mum were baking a special welcome home cake while the baby slept quietly. Suddenly, they heard a strange noise and when they looked into the nursery they saw the baby balancing on top of the crib. She was trying to reach a cuddly toy. Before they could catch her the baby began to wobble and then she fell...! As Millie and Mum rushed forward the baby sat up and laughed. She had fallen safely into the washing basket!

"That's decided!" said Mum. "She must be called Felicity, which means lucky!"

Tyler The Film Bunny

Tyler was watching a film. When it was finished he swaggered in to see Mum.

"Howdy 'ma!" he drawled. "Two fingers of juice, if you please!"

"I don't think so!" replied Mum. "Why are you talking like that?"

"That's how Bronco Bunny, the sheriff in the Western talks!" said Tyler, who acted like a cowboy for the rest of the day.

The next day there was a different film on TV.

"Avast me hearties!" Tyler yelled. "Walk the plank, ye landlubbers! Dad didn't undertand him. "It's pirate-talk, like Captain Silverears!" said Tyler, who acted like the captain until he went to bed.

Next afternoon Grandad came to see Tyler. "Come and watch my favourite film with me!" Grandad said.

Later Mum and Grandad were sitting in the kitchen.

"What was the film you showed Tyler?" she asked.

"Why, it was an old silent movie!" chuckled Grandad.

They didn't hear anything from Tyler for hours!

Non-Stop DJ Dylan

"A big hello out there to all you rockin' rabbits in radio land! This is DJ Dylan with more of your favourite tunes!"

Dylan was presenting his morning music programme. It was very popular but it was hard work. He had to be up very early in the morning before it was even light outside, even after late nights on the air! And even when he wasn't working Dylan had to be up to date with all the latest songs and bands. He would even listen to other radio shows to hear what they were playing. There wasn't a song Dylan hadn't heard or a singer he hadn't seen. But he was starting to look a little greyer than normal!

"It's time you took a holiday!" his boss said. "You're looking tired!"

"What a good idea," agreed Dylan. "What would be the perfect holiday?"

Soon he'd found the perfect spot. A desert island!

"The perfect place!" he smiled, lying back on the beach and listening to the sea. "Not a single radio around!"

Treading the Boards

Erin had always wanted to be an actress and now she was getting the chance. She was the queen in the school play! Everyone had practised hard and Erin was very proud of her costume. She looked very majestic in her golden crown.

The day of the play arrived, and all the parents came to watch.

But soon things started to go wrong! Erin tripped on her cape in the middle of her big speech, she lost a shoe running to greet her guests and when the King began to waltz her round the stage she lost her crown.

The audience roared with laughter. Everyone thought it was meant to be funny!

After the play Mum gave Erin a hug.

"Well done!" she said. "Would you still like to be an actress one day?"

"I think I'd rather be a comedian!" smiled Erin. "I seem to be very good at making people laugh, even when I don't mean to!"

Giants Down Under!

Liam was very excited. His family had flown all the way to Australia. Liam knew that Australia was a very strange place where everything was upside down.

But when he got there he didn't feel upside down.

He also knew that his uncle lived in a bush. Which seemed very odd to him because all the rabbits he knew lived in a thing called a warren!

But when they arrived it didn't look that different from his own home.

"Where's the bush?" he puzzled. His uncle laughed and told him how the big, wild centre of Australia was called 'The Bush' and it didn't mean that he lived inside a plant!

Liam was disappointed. "I was expecting lots of strange things here!" he said. At that moment a giant rabbit bounced by, much taller than the tallest rabbit Liam had ever seen!

"Wow!" shouted Liam. "I didn't know you had giants in Australia?"

"That's not a giant!" smiled Dad. "That's a kangaroo!"

"Nevermind!" said Liam. "That's exciting enough!"

Too Tall And Different

Lewis was the tallest bunny in his class. But he wasn't proud of standing out and being taller than everyone else. He just wanted to be like all his friends. So he would slump his shoulders and make himself as small as possible.

One day there was a school football match. All the pupils went and took a flag with them to support the team. But Lewis's team were losing and then the flagpole broke.

Suddenly Lewis heard a little voice next to him. It was the smallest bunny in the school. He was too small to see the game.

"Climb up on my shoulders," Lewis told him. "Then you can see the game and we can wave the flag high enough so the team can see it too!"

So that's what they did. Having the small bunny on his shoulders was no trouble for Lewis, and anyway, he found that he liked it. He began to feel that he was being useful. He felt even better when the captain of the team saw the flag they were waving and gave them the thumb's up!

Soon Lewis's team had won the game! Lewis smiled.

"Maybe it's good to be different after all!" he thought and held his head up high after that.

The Great Suprendo

Hannah loved magic so she was very excited when her friend had a birthday party with a real magician. But when it was time for the magician to take the stage, he had an announcement to make.

"I'm sorry everyone," he said. "But today's show will be cancelled because my assistant is not very well!"

Hannah leapt up. "I'll help!" she cried. "I know all the magic tricks!"

The magician thought about it, and then he agreed to let Hannah help out. Hannah nearly fainted with excitement!

Hannah and the magician did lots of tricks together and then came the big finale! The magician sawed Hannah in half! Everyone clapped and cheered loudly. It was the loudest applause the magician had ever had!

"I'm very grateful to you!" the magician told Hannah. "How can I thank you?"

"Well," said Hannah, "What I'd really like is if you would train me to be a proper magician myself!"

And that's what happened. Years later, Hannah was performing to happy crowds. She called herself the 'Great Suprendo'!

The Snow Bunny Prize

It had been snowing hard and so all the bunnies agreed to have a snow bunny building contest. Mr Fuzzylop said that the best snow bunny would win a special prize. Everyone was very excited and set to work right away.

Harriet and Julia tried very hard to make the perfect snow bunny but they just couldn't get it right.

"That looks more like a snow monster than a snow bunny!" jeered Cameron. But Harriet had an idea. When it was time for judging Julia was nowhere to be seen. Mr Fuzzylop was very impressed with Harriet's snow bunny. It was exactly the right shape and was even complete with whiskers!

"Wait a second!" cried Mr Fuzzylop. "You can't make whiskers out of snow!" The secret was out. Harriet patted her snow bunny, and the snow fell off… to reveal Julia! She had been the snow bunny! Mr Fuzzylop frowned, and then he laughed and laughed!

And although they didn't win, Mr Fuzzylop gave them both a carrot bar for making him laugh so much!

What To Do With A Book

"Can I please borrow a book?" Phoebe asked Grandad Bunny. His house was full of books from the ceiling to the floors!

"Of course!" replied Grandad. "What kind of book would you like?"

"A big one please!" said Phoebe.

So Grandad fetched a large book and gave it to her.

"I think you might like this one!" he said.

"Thank you!" said Phoebe disappearing. But in a minute she was back.

"Can I swap this for a bigger book, please?" she asked.

Grandad was confused. He went and got the biggest, thickest book he had.

"Are you sure?" he asked. "This book is very heavy for a little bunny like you!"

"Yes, I'm sure!" said Phoebe, leading him to the kitchen. Then she put the book on the floor and stood on it.

"See? Now I can reach the cookies up on that shelf!"

Dominic The Daredevil

Dominic the Daredevil travelled all over the world in search of danger, excitement and adventure. He climbed the highest mountain, dived in shark-infested waters, caved deep under the ground and did lots of other daring feats! He was the bravest bunny and nothing could stop him! He spent his holidays racing cars or trekking through jungle or desert. He was everyone's hero!

One day, after another exciting adventure, a famous television reporter visited Dominic.

"I have a special job for you!" said the reporter.

"What is it?" asked Dominic. "A flight into space? Swimming the Bermuda Triangle? I'm up for anything!"

"Not quite," replied the reporter. "I'd like to interview you for my TV show. You can appear before your millions of fans!"

Dominic turned very pale and green. The truth was, Dominic was incredibly shy, and didn't like talking to people, or talking about himself.

"Erm… no thanks." he said. "I don't think I could.

Can't I wrestle a rabbit-eating tiger instead?"

George's Rosebushes

George was a famous gardener. He could grow almost anything but he loved roses best.

"I wish I could grow blue roses," he sighed. "They would look so beautiful in my garden!" But try as he might, George had no success.

One day his brother, Sinbad, came to visit after a long sea voyage.

"You're in luck!" Sinbad told him. "On my travels I collected lots of rare flowers. One of them was a blue rosebush!"

Sinbad brought round the bush. George was very pleased and planted it straight away. "Enjoy it!" said Sinbad, and set off on another voyage.

That night it rained very hard. In the morning George had a shock.

"My roses have turned white!" he exclaimed. There were big splashes of blue paint under the bush!

"My brother's terrible!" George laughed. "Just wait until he gets back!"

Fur, Scales Or Feathers?

Owen loved watching nature programmes but something puzzled him.

"Mum, why do we bunnies have fur? Why not scales like lizards have? Or feathers like the birds have?"

"We'd look very funny without fur!" Mum laughed as she made the bed. "And we'd certainly be cold!"

Owen thought hard. "Lizards have scales, don't they? But they need sunshine to warm them up. And there's not much sunshine round here. Mum's right, we would be too cold! But why not feathers…?"

He picked up a pillow for Mum but it caught on the corner of the nightstand. There was a ripping noise and suddenly feathers exploded all over the room!

"Atishoo!" Feathers tickled his nose and made him sneeze! Others went down his shirt and made Owen laugh and laugh.

"I know why we don't have feathers," giggled Owen. "They tickle too much!"

Jayden The Magician

When Connor got a book of magic tricks for his birthday he tried them out on everybody. Soon the whole neighbourhood had seen them!

One day a family of bunnies moved in next door. One was called Jayden and Connor decided to show him his tricks. First he did lots of clever card tricks and then he made a carrot appear from nowhere.

"Can you make a cookie vanish?" asked Jayden.

"Of course!" said Connor proudly.

"So can I!" said Jayden, asking his mum for two cookies, one for Connor.

"Watch" said Connor and with a wave of his hand the cookie had disappeared!

"Now it's my turn!" smiled Jayden.

"You won't be able to do it!" frowned Connor.

"Yes I can! It's easy!" said Jayden. He put the cookie in his mouth and ate it.

"Abracadabra!" he laughed, "and it's gone!"

Nathan Forgets, Again!

Nathan was always forgetting to do things.

He forgot to brush his teeth.

He forgot to tidy his room.

He even forgot to bring his favourite toy car in from the garden until his brother brought it in, all rusty and muddy from the rain.

One day Nathan was invited to go to the beach with his friend Toby. He searched everywhere for his swimsuit and found it under his bed. Then he ran downstairs and put it by the door.

"I'm ready to go!" he said. He picked up his lunchbox and rushed out of the burrow.

After lunch Toby's dad suggested a swim. "It's lovely and warm!"
So Nathan looked for his swimsuit.

"Oh no!" he cried "It's still by the front door!"
While everyone else swam in the sea Nathan had to sit on the beach all alone.

"I'll never forget anything again!" he said. And he never did.

Mason's Moving Day

Mason's family were moving burrows. Everything was packed up in boxes. Everybody was ready to go, except Mason. He didn't want to move. He liked their old, damp burrow. He liked the hole under the floorboards where he could hide his secrets. He would miss the garden and his favourite big tree.

When it was time to go Mason hid.

"I'm not going!" he thought.

But Dad found him.

"I promise you'll like it!" Dad told Mason.

"No I won't!" Mason sobbed. "It won't be as good as our old burrow!"

The new burrow was warm and dry and Mason had a room of his very own.

Even better there was a huge garden with lots of huge trees.

When Mason woke up the next day he couldn't help smiling.

"I will miss our old home," he thought. "But I do like this one!"

Billy's Lettuce Patch

Billy was always hungry! He liked to crunch on juicy, orange carrots. He loved golden corn. But most of all Billy loved to eat crisp, green lettuces.

One day Dad gave Billy a patch of garden. "You can grow whatever you like!" Dad told him.

Billy looked at the square of newly dug earth. Beside it was a green watering can and a trowel.

"I think I know what I would like to grow!" Billy said. He dug a little trench, sowed his seeds and watered them everyday. He even did the weeding.

By the summer Billy's garden was full of big, fat lettuces. He had so many he decided to have a big party with all his friends.

"I grew the lettuces myself!" Billy proudly told everyone.

And everyone agreed they were the best lettuces they had ever eaten!

I Hate Being Small!

Reuben was four and was only small. Everyone told him so.

Reuben wished he was big. He couldn't reach the kitchen cupboard to get some carrot cookies. He couldn't reach the sink to wash his paws. Mum always had to get him a stool to stand on.

"I hate being small, Mum!" said Reuben.

"Can you tie your shoelaces?" Mum asked.

"Yes," said Reuben.

"And can you eat by yourself with a knife and fork?"

"Yes," said Reuben.

"And can you paint a picture and count to twenty?"

"Yes I can," said Reuben.

"Well then," Mum said. "Being big is all about learning to do things yourself and you can do lots of things on your own!"

Reuben thought. "I can do lots of things!" he said. "And I'll keep learning too! Maybe being four isn't so little after all!"

Sophie's Perfect Pet

Tilly had a goldfish. Sara had a tiny mouse. But Sophie didn't have a pet at all and she wanted one more than anything!

"You can't have one just yet," said her mum.

"A pet takes a lot of work!" said her dad. "You have to feed and clean it. You can have one when you're older!"

One day Mum gave Sophie a box.

"Is it a pet?" Sophie asked excitedly.

"Sort of!" Mum replied. "Why don't you have a look?"

So Sophie peered inside. It was soft and furry and looked just like a baby rabbit.

"It's a glove puppet!" said Dad. "Put it on your paw."

Sophie did so. She made the puppet move, cuddled it and took it everywhere. It didn't take up much room and she didn't even need to feed or clean it!

"Thank you!" she said. "It's my practise pet…
until I'm old enough for a real one."

A Very Hoppy Ending!

Mrs Angora wore glasses and walked very slowly with a stick. She was so old her fur had turned silver and white.

One day Mum arranged for Elliot, Rose and Lexie to visit Mrs Angora. Elliot didn't want to go.

"Old people are boring!" he said, "And I bet Mrs Angora is boring too!"

During their visit Mrs Angora gave them all a delicious slice of cake.

"Thank you!" said Rose and Lexie.

But Elliot wouldn't take any and sat sulking.

"You are grumpy!" said Mrs Angora. "Maybe I should tell you a joke to cheer you up? What kind of book does a rabbit like at bedtime?"

"We don't know!" Rose and Lexie giggled.

"One with a hoppy ending," replied Mrs Angora.

Rose and Lexie burst out laughing and Elliot couldn't help joining in.

"You see!" Rose said later. "Old people aren't boring at all!"

Elliot was Mrs Angora's most regular visitor after that!

Dad's Birthday Present

It was Dad's birthday and Alex and Mum decided to buy him a running machine.

"Dad will love this!" said Mum. "He keeps saying he wants to get fit!"

The day before Dad's birthday Mum went out to get Dad's carrot and cabbage birthday cake.

"Don't play with the running machine while I'm away!" she said to Alex. But Alex couldn't resist.

"I'll just have a look!" he thought. "I wonder how it works?"

He pressed a red button on the handle and the machine started up.

"Well now it's working I might as well have a little go," he thought. So he climbed on and started running. But the faster he ran the faster the machine went. Alex could hardly breathe.

When Mum came home she said, "You do look thin and tired, Alex! Never mind! You can have some cake when Dad comes in!"

How Do I Go To Sleep?

"Night night" said Mum tucking Leah into bed. "Sleep tight!"

"But I'm not tired!" moaned Leah.

"Well the best way to get to sleep is to count squirrels," replied Mum. "Why don't you try that?"

So Leah started counting. "One, two, three, four…"

"Five!" said a tiny voice. Leah turned over and found a tiny squirrel on her pillow. "Everyone's always asleep before they reach me!" said Five. "You must be very awake! Why don't we go exploring? I promise I'll look after you!"

So Five showed Leah how to climb a tree and they leapt gracefully among the branches. Then they jumped from one tree to another. It was like flying! Suddenly Leah heard her mum calling. "Leah! Leah!"

"I think it's time for you to go home!" said Five.

The next thing Leah knew was Mum pulling back the covers.

"Leah! Time to get up!" she said, "Did you have a nice dream?"

A Bathtime Adventure

"I name this ship the HMS Bunny!" announced Toby. "And with me as her captain we will set sail to many exotic lands!"

With a splash, the HMS Bunny slid gracefully into the water.

"Raise the mainsail!" Toby ordered. "Hop to it men!"

The water began to grow rough and the boat struggled to stay afloat.

"All hands on deck!" yelled Captain Toby. "There a storm coming! Captain Toby has never failed his crew yet!"

Soon a huge wave broke across the deck sending spray flying. The HMS Bunny dipped and rose, almost capsizing.

Suddenly, Mum appeared with a towel.

"You naughty bunny!" she exclaimed. "You've splashed water all over the bathroom floor again!"

"Sorry Mum!" Toby grinned. "I was playing at being a ship's captain!"

"Well maybe next time Captain Toby will choose calmer waters!" laughed Mum. "Otherwise he might be sent to the galley to peel potatoes instead!"

First Day At School

It was the day Grace was going to start at Cottontail Playschool. She had a brand new blue dress and a special pencil case shaped like a butterfly. But at breakfast Mum noticed that Grace, who usually talked all the time, had gone very quiet. At the school gate she held on to Mum's hand very tightly and wouldn't let go.

"Please don't leave me!" she said and so Mum agreed to stay for a little bit.

Everyone sat in a circle and heard a story about a little rabbit in a blue coat. Then they all painted pictures of the story and the teacher put the pictures up on the wall.

Grace was shy at first, but when her picture got a special gold star from the teacher, she really started enjoying herself. And she didn't even notice when Mum tiptoed out of the room.

Later when Mum came to pick her up, Grace just couldn't stop talking!

The Birthday Surprise

Tom was very excited. Today was his birthday and he had hardly slept thinking of the presents, cake and big party he would have. When it was time to get up he raced downstairs.

But when he got there everything was as it was everyday. No presents, no cards and no sign of a party.

"Morning Tom," said Mum as she put down a bowl of carrot flakes. "Get dressed please. After breakfast we're going shopping."

Tom munched his breakfast and waited for someone to wish him happy birthday but no one did. Dad read his paper and Mum tidied the kitchen. It seemed everyone had forgotten his birthday!
Dad and Mum headed to the shops with Tom trudging sadly behind.

"Surprise!" yelled Mum and Dad, and all Tom's friends jumped out of hiding at Bunny's Burger Bar. "Happy Birthday! We haven't forgotten at all!"

Share And Share Alike

Grandma had given Alicia and Zak a big red ball for Christmas and told them to share. They never did though and they often argued about it.

"It's mine!" shouted Alicia

"No, I want the ball!" screamed back Zak.

In the garden they pulled it back and forth. They were so busy arguing that they didn't notice how close to the river they were. Suddenly the ball slipped away from them. It rolled away and fell in the water.

"Oh no!" wailed Alicia "Now it's lost forever!"

Luckily Ollie otter was swimming nearby.

"Who dropped this ball?" he asked.

"It's ours!" said Zak. "We were fighting but we promise to play nicely now!"

Ollie tossed the ball to Alicia. "Here you go," he said "but remember to share! It's much more fun to play together than all alone!" And it was!

Dragon In The Garden

The bunnies were playing happily outside when the ground where Hollie stood began to shake. A mound of earth grew up quite suddenly in front of her.

"What do you think it is?" asked Francesca.

Hollie said it had to be a dragon. She was reading a story about a dragon that lived deep under the ground.

Everyone looked at the mound. Then Louie took a stick and tapped it. There was a snuffling, shuffling sound from deep inside.

"It's definitely a dragon!" the others agreed, "and it sounds hungry!"

Soon a small black face appeared and two tiny beady eyes blinked in the sunlight. It was Morgan the mole. "Hello?" he called.

"Did someone knock?"

But everyone had gone. No-one wanted to be the dragon's dinner!

Splish! Splash! Splosh!

It was raining very heavily as Joe walked home from school. But Joe had his shiny blue anorak, green wellies and had his red umbrella with him so he didn't care! He splashed in the puddles, kicking up the water. Then he tried jumping over the puddles. Sometimes he would land right in the middle of one but because of his coat and boots he stayed nice and dry.

He was nearly home when he saw a HUGE puddle and he couldn't resist. He ran up to it and jumped…

Splash! The puddle was much deeper than Joe had thought and suddenly he was up to his waist in water. It ran into his boots and soaked through his trousers, even his pants were wet!

And so it was one very wet bunny that went home that night! Joe always thought twice about jumping in puddles after that!

Harley's Fantastic Dreams

Harley always had fantastic dreams. "Last night I dreamed that I was zooming into space in a carrot-shaped rocket!" he told his friends. "And the moon was made of lettuce!"

The next day Harley was asleep in the garden when Reece and Sara came round.

"I was just dreaming that I slid down the rainbow and found a pot of golden corn!" said Harley licking his lips.

"Do you want to come and see what we are doing his afternoon?" asked Reece but Harley was already snoring again and so they tiptoed away.

When Harley at last woke up he saw a princess and a knight.

"I must still be dreaming!" gasped Harley.

But suddenly he realised it was his friends in costume.

"We're putting on a play. Would you like to see it?" they said, smiling a welcoming smile.

"I wouldn't dream of missing it!" laughed Harley.

Hide And Seek Fun!

Aidan and his friends were playing hide and seek and Aidan knew just the place to hide. He sneaked away and hid under some brambles at the edge of the wood.

"No-one will think to look for me here!" he thought.

And he was right. He waited and waited but no-one came. It started to get dark and Aidan began to wonder if he had found too good a hiding place! There were scary shadows and strange noises. Aidan started to imagine there were all sorts of horrible things waiting to get him!

The noises got louder and Aidan tried to make himself as small as possible. Suddenly he heard a voice he knew.

"Dad!" he cried springing out of his hiding place. "You found me when no-one else could!"

Dad gave him a hug. "The wood's no place for a little rabbit after dark! Come on, lets go home!"

Logan Learns To Write

Logan had started school. He couldn't wait for storytime, sitting on the mat listening to teacher read. He loved painting class. He even liked maths and could count all the way to twenty! But there was one thing Logan wasn't looking forward to and that was learning to write. The whole class had been practising the alphabet but Logan was new. He was sure he wouldn't be able to put the letters together to make a whole word!

When the big day came Logan was very nervous. His mum bought him a special green pencil with red stripes.

"Everyone get out your pencil and paper," said Miss Lop. When Logan took out his pencil he felt a bit braver. Miss Lop came round and showed him how to write his name - L O G A N. Logan felt very proud.

That night he showed his mum. "Look what I did at school!" he cried and he wrote his name over and over again!

"There now!" said his mum. "Look at you, writing like you've always been able to do it! You're a very good boy!" And she gave him a big hug and his favourite dinner - roasted carrots and cabbage mash!

A Very Peculiar Dream

It was getting late, but Madeleine could not get to sleep. She tossed and turned, tried counting squirrels and even went and got some warm milk. Nothing worked.

"I wonder what would happen if I stayed awake all night," she thought.

Suddenly an orange moth appeared and said, "Bunnies always fall asleep sooner or later. There's no doubt about it!"

"But I don't feel at all tired!" said Madeleine.

She rubbed her eyes and found a large silver crocodile and a green duck standing at the end of her bed.

"I bet I'm the first bunny to stay awake all night!" said Madeleine.

"Bunnies always fall asleep sooner or later!" said the crocodile and the duck.

"I don't think I will!" said Madeleine.

The next thing she knew her mum was opening the curtains.

"I think I've been awake all night!" Madeleine said.

Mum laughed. "I don't think you have! Not unless you snore while you're awake!"

Madeleine was a bit embarassed but then she remembered the funny animals in her dreams and had to laugh.

Ben's Surprise Swim!

Ben looked down at the river. He could see the fish darting about. He wished he could join them swimming all day in the warm water instead of having to do boring rabbit-type things on dry land. The only problem was… Ben couldn't swim.

He leaned even further over the edge. Splash! The water was freezing and the weeds were slimy between his paws. He coughed and spluttered but eventually climbed back onto the bank.

Ben had to squelch the whole way home, cold and wet. Weeds hung from his fur and tail. He didn't want to be a fish anymore!

Mum had a lovely hot bath ready for him when he got home.

"I'll book a swimming lesson for you," she said. "The pool is warm and there won't be any weeds to get in your way!"

Soon Ben was swimming just like a fish. But he never tried to go swimming in the weedy river again!

What Do You Do Best?

Ashton and his friends decided to have a competition. The first event was tree climbing. Ashton found it harder than he had thought. Then it was Joel Squirrel's turn. In the blink of an eye he was at the top of the tree, waving down at the others!

"I win!" he called. "Climbing is what squirrels do best!"

Then Ellis Bat suggested they see who could hang upside down longest. It made Ashton very dizzy and Ellis clearly won.

"Hanging upside down is what bats do best!" Ellis said.

The third event was to see who could hide the longest. Kian Mouse won, he was the smallest and could find the best hiding places.

"Hiding is what mice do best!" smiled Kian.

Ashton was fed up by now. He hadn't won anything!

"I've an idea!" he said. "Why don't we have a hopping race?"

This time Ashton won easily. After all, rabbits hop very well indeed!

Zack Learns A Lesson

Zack thought playing tricks on people was very funny indeed. The only problem was that his friends didn't agree!

"Duck!" he shouted to Theo.

"Why?" said Theo, quickly crouching down and looking around.

"No, Imogen Duck. She's over there!" laughed Zack.

But later that day his friends decided to get their own back.

"Come and look through Finlay Fox's telescope!" said Ellie. "There's something funny at the end of it!"

Zack peered through. "I can't see anything funny!" he said. But as he turned around everyone else burst into laughter. When Zack looked in a mirror he saw there was a black mark all around his eye.

"It's only grease!" giggled Theo. "I told you there was something funny at the end of the telescope!"

But Zack had learnt his lesson and he never played a trick on anybody else again.

Scared Of The Dark

Nettie was scared of the dark so her mum bought her a special night-light for when she went to bed. But Nettie didn't like the way the night-light made her room look. It cast scary shadows that looked like monsters and ghosts! When Mum came in to wish her good night she was still awake.

"You know, shadows don't have to be scary," Mum told her. "You can even make shadows of your own!" She held her paws up in front of the night-light and showed Nettie how to make a bird-shaped shadow on the wall.

"See?" Mum said. "Why don't you make some before you go to sleep?" So Nettie made more shadows with her paws. She made a moose and then a bunny shadow and felt much better about being in the dark. And before she knew it, she was fast asleep.

Andrew's New Shoes

Andrew felt very left out. All the other bunnies in his class had fashionable trainers and he didn't have any trainers at all. All he had were old brown shoes.

"I want some trainers!" he told Dad. "A cool, new pair!"
But no matter how much Andrew asked the answer was always the same.

"I'm sorry Andrew but trainers are much too expensive! You'll just have to make do with your old shoes for now!"

When it was time for school Andrew looked everywhere for his shoes but he couldn't find them anywhere. In their place were some shiny red shoes with sunshine yellow laces.

"I painted you old shoes to brighten them up!" said Mum.
Everyone at school thought Andrew's shoes were even better than trainers and Andrew was soon the coolest bunny around!

The Special Surprise

Lauren's most special possession was a magic cupboard. She had bought it from an old man who said he was a wizard. If Lauren wanted anything, all she had to do was whisper a magic spell through the keyhole. When she opened the cupboard there it would be. Everyone thought Lauren's cupboard was wonderful. But her friend Leon was very jealous.

When Lauren went out he sneaked into Lauren's house and tiptoed over to the cupboard. Then he whispered through the keyhole, "Give me a special surprise!" Suddenly the doors opened and a hand grabbed Leon. It pulled him inside, flew into the air, soared over the duckpond, and then dropped him in it with a splash. Then the cupboard flew home and was back in its corner before Lauren got home. That cupboard certainly did give Leon a surprise he didn't forget!

A Very Snowy Day!

When winter came the bunnies all stayed inside in the warm. The rain poured down, the sky was dark and a freezing wind blew. Every morning was gloomy and grey and it made the bunnies very grumpy.

"We hate winter!" they cried. "We want it to be summer again!"

One morning though the bunnies woke up to find the world covered with snow.

"Hurray!" they yelled tumbling down the stairs and out the front door.

They played in the snow all day. They made snow bunnies, had snowball fights and went sledging. By dinnertime they were cold and tired but very happy.

"We love winter!" they said. "We don't want it to ever be summer again!"

A Rabbit Restaurant

"I'm going to open a restaurant," Sienna told her friend Niamh Squirrel. "Would you like to help me run it?"

"Only if I can be the cook!" said Niamh.

On the opening night Niamh was all set up in the kitchen. When the first customers arrived Sienna was the waitress and took their orders. Then she ran into the kitchen.

"Two carrot soups and one carrot salad, please!" she told Niamh.

Niamh quickly got to work. "Coming right up!" she replied.

More customers arrived.

"One carrot juice, four carrot casseroles and two carrot cakes please!"

Soon the restaurant was full and Niamh was very busy.

"Another carrot pie please!" said Sienna.

"I'm fed up of cooking carrots!" said Niamh, who had not had a chance to leave the kitchen all evening. "Why don't our customers order anything else?"

"Did I forget to tell you?" said Sienna. "This a restaurant for rabbits!"

The Surprise Party!

Zoe, Harvey and Max were planning Zoe's birthday party.

"I think I'd like to have a fancy dress party," said Zoe.

"That's a great idea!" said Harvey "What about film characters?"

Zoe thought hard for a moment. Then she remembered her favourite film, 'Sleeping Bunny'.

"I'll be the princess in that!" she cried. "It's the perfect costume, especially as it's my party!"

Harvey loved Westerns and so he decided to be a cowboy.

But Max couldn't think of a single idea and as the party drew closer every other costume idea was quickly taken.

On the day of the party there was a knock at the door. Zoe answered it and yelled with fright.

"Grrr!" yelled Max "It's only me! Everyone else was coming as a hero so I thought I'd be a baddie!"

"Fancy coming as a fox!" Harvey laughed. "Good idea, Max!"

A Brand New Friend

Abbie was feeling very lonely. She had just started a new school and didn't know anybody. There were so many bunnies and she felt much too shy to go up to one of the big groups and say hello. When playtime came all the other bunnies seemed to have someone to play with. Abbie grumpily went and sat under a tree all alone. Soon another bunny sat next to her. She looked miserable too.

At last Abbie got up the courage and decided to talk to the bunny.

"What's wrong?" Abbie asked shyly.

"I haven't got anyone to play with," the bunny replied. "I'm new here."

"So am I!" laughed Abbie "Why don't we be friends?"

The other bunny jumped up. "My name's Izzy! What's yours?"

"Abbie," said Abbie. "What would you like to play?"

Abbie forgot all about being lonely and soon had a new best friend!

What A Mess, Vicky!

Mum was taking some shopping to Mrs Rex, their elderly next door neighbour.

"Please can you look after your little sister Vicky for me?" she asked Alex. "I won't be long but you know how she can get into trouble!"

Alex said he would but soon he was tired of his little sister following him around. He wanted to play his own games without her messing them up.

"Go and find your own game!" Alex shouted. "I want to play on my own!" Vicky wandered off and Alex forgot all about her.

About lunchtime Alex remembered Vicky. With horror he followed a trail of mud from the garden and found her.

"What a mess!" Alex thought. "I had better clear this up before Mum gets home!" He had to work really hard but he finished just in time!

Alex never forgot about his sister after that and was always careful to keep her entertained. After all you never knew what kind of trouble she could get into!

The Treehouse Home

When Skye Squirrel went to visit Paige Bunny she was busily mopping up water from her burrow.

"The storm last night made such a mess!" Paige told her. "The wind blew all the rain under my front door!"

"If you lived in a tree like mine you wouldn't have that problem!" laughed Skye. "It always stays dry!"

"I never heard of rabbits living in trees," said Paige "But I'll give it a go!"

So Paige went to stay at Skye's. As she climbed up the stairs it did seem a very long way up. But at the top Skye's home was nice and cosy and not a single drop of rain had got inside.

Suddenly dark clouds filled the sky and there was a great gust of wind. The tree swayed and rocked.

"I think I'll stay in my burrow after all!" said Paige. "Your home might stay drier but mine doesn't move!"

The Hop-Hop Race!

"I can hop much further than you!" boasted Robin Rabbit to Christopher Frog.

"I bet you can't!" croaked Christopher.

So they had a competition to see who could hop the furthest. Robin won easily.

"I bet I can hop faster than you too!" he said. "Let's race around the field!"

Of course Robin won that too which just made his bragging worse!

Eventually Christopher couldn't take it anymore.

"I know somewhere that you can't hop!" he smiled. He hopped onto a large lily pad floating in the nearby stream. Without thinking Robin tried to follow. Splash! Robin was much heavier than Christopher. He was soaked! Christopher started laughing and soon Robin did too.

"It serves me right for showing off," he said, "but now I'd better hop off home to get dry!"

The Prettiest Picture

Madison was very good at painting and had pictures in lots of galleries. She had just finished painting a view of the river when Taylor came along. As usual Taylor was crunching on a big, juicy carrot, and it made Madison feel quite hungry!

"I wish I could paint as well as you!" Taylor said.

"I'm sure you could if you tried!" Madison replied. "Why don't you have a go with my paints while I go home for some lunch?"

"Do you really think I could paint as well as you?" Taylor asked.

"Of course!" said Madison "You just have to paint something beautiful and this view is very beautiful indeed!"

Taylor smiled, popped his half-eaten carrot in his pocket, and started to paint. A little later Madison was back.

"I've just finished!" Taylor told her. "What do you think? It's the most beautiful thing I can think of. A yummy giant carrot!"

Noah The Astronaut

"Preparing for take off. Three... two... one... lift off!"

Noah was going to be one of the first rabbits on the Moon. From his spaceship he looked out at the stars whizzing by. Below was the tiny, faraway Earth.

Suddenly, Noah could hear ground control calling him.

"Noah! Noah! Pay attention Noah!"

Noah jumped and opened his eyes. His teacher, Mrs Sable, was standing by his desk and didn't look very happy.

"I'm sorry!" said Noah sitting up and looking at the documentary on space the class was watching. "I must have been dreaming! I was an astronaut travelling into space!"

"Dear me!" laughed Mrs Sable. "Well you won't ever get to go into space if you don't listen in class. Astronauts have to be very clever!"

Noah worked very hard from then on and guess what... he grew up to be a famous astronaut after all!

Beautiful Bunny Ears

Jasmine had long ears. They were so long that they often flopped in her eyes and she was always bumping into things!

All the other bunnies had small ears. Many of them made fun of Jasmine.

"Big Ears! Big Ears!" they jeered.

"I wish I had small ears like yours!" Jasmine told her best friend Meg. "Then I would be the same as everyone else and no-one could make fun of me!"

But Meg thought Jasmine's ears were lovely. Suddenly Meg had an idea. She went inside and brought out a big box of ribbons, all the colours of the rainbow. Then she took the most beautiful pink ribbon and tied it around Jasmine's head with a big bow.

"There!" she said. "Your ears will stay out of your eyes now!"

Now the other rabbits all wear ribbons just like Jasmine!